Note for readers

The Sunset Chronicles is a monthly sci fi serial. Think of it like a series, much like you'd get on your favourite tv streaming service. There are seasons, split up into episodes (five per season). Each episode is designed to be read in roughly two hours, though fast readers may blast through them even quicker, and those who like to really get stuck into the story may take longer. They're intended to be thrilling and exciting, and are released regularly each month so that you can keep up with the story even if you have a hectic schedule. And who doesn't, these days? It's perfect for if you want to slip some space horror into your lunch break, or if you want to binge it of an evening.

If you've come to this book first, please check out episode one, *Last Light*, which is available in ebook and print.

Also, although *The Sunset Chronicles* is a story that stretches from the ice moon of Europa to every corner of the globe, its author remains English. As such, international readers should note that spellings are of the UK variation of English, so if you see a typo, it must be because of that.

If you're in the UK and you see a typo, it must be your imagination.

SEASON ONE: EPISODE TWO

SUNSET CHRONICLES

FAULT & FRACTURE

PAUL STEPHENSON

HOLLOW STONE

Chapter One

One look at Walker's shuttle told Judd the old man hadn't been on the level with him. It was worth more than the other private shuttles docked at the Key put together. There was no way a man who could afford to travel in this kind of luxury would vacation at such a third-rate shithole. He couldn't have come all this way just for him, surely?

Rather than confront Walker, Judd climbed aboard. It was, he had to admit, both flattering and exciting to think this all might be for him.

The ride back to Earth was as thrilling. The blue green marble hurtled toward them at a speed inconceivable to Judd. As the marble filled their viewfinder, his stomach did backflips of nausea and excitement.

Walker and Judd barely spoke. Walker was apologetic for the lack of attention, but he had seemingly endless work to do, conversations to have. For a man of his age, Judd had never seen anyone work so hard; which again played into Judd's feeling this had been a setup.

But how? Judd had never registered as a teep, had never shown it to anyone. Sure, there might have been a record somewhere from a teacher who had suspicions, but he'd passed the test. So how did this important teep know enough about him to travel to the moon and back?

Whatever the answer, Judd let it slide. He'd made his decision, and he could hardly turn back now. They landed at the Port of Paris, where a pod whisked them to Walker's private glide. On board, Walker started his calls once more. Whoever was on the other end of the phone bore the full brunt of a missive about the barely functioning British government and their inability to get their infrastructure up and running.

Two operatives met them at the glide, presumably teeps, both clad in clothes so nondescript they actually stood out. They took up seats in the glide behind Walker, saying nothing either to their boss, or to Judd, whose existence they seemed not to have noticed.

Tiredness washed over Judd as the north of France turned to marshlands, giving way to the murky brown of what had once been the English Channel. He drifted, his thoughts turning from excitement to dread about where they might be going. Walker hadn't even told him their destination, but he assumed it was Whitby, wherever the hell that was.

Judd heard about the flooding of Europe when he was a kid, but in America coverage of the Great Flood was more focused on the impacts on the eastern seaboard. Europe became a footnote, although the devastation there had been greater. But nothing could prepare him for the devastation as they flew over the channel.

They passed over London, or what little remained of it. The city was gone, its remaining landmarks sticking out of stagnant brown water, their surfaces green and mossy. The whole place looked sick, stricken. In the distance where water met the land, the city resumed. On the horizon, so huge they blotted out the sky, stood a dozen or so huge black towers, ugly great scars on the landscape.

'Such a waste of a city,' Walker said. He too stared down at the devastation. 'When I was a young man I came to London. It was the most exciting city I'd ever seen. There was so much going on, every single day. And the food.... Now, every time I go home, I have to pass over its carcass. It's like the new government wants to shove it in your face what a shitty stick they got handed.'

'Why do you live here, if you don't mind me asking?'

He smirked. 'Because the place has still got class.'

In stark contrast to the view, a server brought out a silver tray bearing each a steak dinner. Real steak. Judd had never tried it before, and it made his stomach ache once he'd gotten through it.

The combination of meat, lack of sleep, and the endless sprawling murk below took its toll and Judd drifted off to sleep. Incredibly, for a man with one century and a quarter of another under his belt, Walker didn't seem at all tired.

By the time the marshlands of the drowned lands gave way to the surviving cities of Birmingham and Leeds, Judd fought to stay awake. The once green and pleasant lands were mostly fallow and brown, blighted by the Mar the same as everywhere else. The temperature in the glide tumbled. As they passed over rolling hills, the ground below them became increasingly dotted with ice and snow.

'Where are we going?' Judd asked, finally.

'Whitby,' Walker replied, his voice full of pride. 'Well, not quite. The old town is gone, swept away by the waters, but we have a complex in the hills. It's a beautiful part of the world, the Esk Valley. It's become a home to us, and to others like us.' He peered below, where the last of the day's light shone over majestically rolling hills covered in a green which didn't seem to have survived anywhere else in the country. 'These are the moors,' he said. 'Did you ever read Wuthering Heights?'

Judd shook his head.

'Shame,' Walker said, and turned back to look out of the window once more.

Judd peered down at the view below. The glide slowed, allowing him to see more of the view. It was breathtaking. The glide hugged the contours of rolling hills. There was little in the way of human habitation, save for crumbling old farmhouses, mostly abandoned and going to seed. Picturesque villages remained, clinging desperately to the sides of hills as they tried to weather the storm of irrelevance in a world that no longer needed the countryside.

They cleared one particularly large hill; the valley leading up to it dammed up, a huge swath of concrete cutting the valley in two. Beyond, spread across the valley like a sprawl of chrome and metal, was what looked somewhere between a town and an industrial estate.

Judd leaned forward and pressed his nose against the glass.

'Impressive, isn't it?' Walker said, smiling.

'This is yours?'

'Not mine—ours. You're a part of it, now. But I am a kind of unofficial leader here.'

'Leader of what?' Judd asked. Walker smirked and Judd's gaze went back to the glass. 'Are there going to be others like me down there?'

'Yes, but most of the people working there don't even know what the base is for. To them it's a government facility.'

The glide came in at pace over the buildings, heading for a landing pad in a rare spot of empty land next to a pretty little river running through the central square. It had been a good half an hour since they'd seen habitation bigger than a few houses, but this looked like it could house and sustain hundreds. It was completely self-contained, with the dam at both ends of the valley keeping the waters out, save for the small trickle of the stream. The vegetation here was different, too, with lush greens all around, and a long hill filled with vegetable patches and animals. Judd had never seen a cow before, but there they were, mingling with sheep and other creatures he'd only seen in books. Farmers worked the sides of the valley that stretched up and along for some time.

'How...' Judd asked, but the glide touched down, and Walker was already wheeling his chair to the exit.

'Come on,' Walker said.

The air outside stank of sulphur and manure, strong enough to catch in the back of Judd's throat. In two years he'd breathed nothing but recycled air, purified of toxins and endlessly sanitised. This was his first lungful of real, unfiltered air, and it tasted like shit. He tried to cover up his distaste with limited success.

If Walker noticed his discomfort, he didn't react. He wheeled over to a large chrome door built onto a structure which looked much older than the rest of the complex. The crumbling stone walls were at least a hundred years old. It must have been a huge farmhouse at some point, albeit one jazzed up with modern windows and a communications mast that wouldn't have looked out of place on the side of a space station.

A woman came out to greet them, nearly as old as Walker himself. She held a pad in her hand and strode across to greet Walker. Judd couldn't hear their greeting over the sound of the glide, rising away to its next trip, but it was businesslike. Formal.

The woman and Walker turned and headed back toward the compound, leaving Judd stranded on the tarmac. As the engines of the glide powered back up to leave, he ran to catch up.

There weren't as many people milling about as Judd had assumed by the scale of the place, but it was getting late, judging by the slowly sinking sun. According to his body clock, he should already be asleep. He tried to recall what earth time the moon kept, but between running after two pensioners and his tiredness, he couldn't remember.

They entered through wide open glass doors into what looked like a hotel lobby. There were more people inside, bustling about, looking busy or standing sentry. They wore uniforms of blue, discreet enough to look like casual wear if there hadn't been so many of them standing in one place. These people looked Judd over as one, each stepping forward slightly in anticipation until Walker waved them away.

Parts of the building had grown up around an old stone-brick farmhouse, but the ancient gave way to ultra-modern and clean lines, all glass and chrome. With the amount of window space, the entire building filled with what remained of the setting sun, with automatic lights powering up to augment the fading light.

Walker turned to face Judd. 'Judd, I hope you will excuse me, but there are matters requiring my urgent attention. I had hoped to give you a tour, but I can send someone round shortly. Can I ask you to find your own way to your room?'

'Uh...'

'Down this corridor, third door on the left, then seventh door along,' the elderly woman added, the first words she'd spoken to him.

Walker looked him up and down. 'There'll be some clothes in there. You can freshen up a bit.'

Without waiting for a response, Walker spun in his chair and headed off down a different corridor, followed by the woman. Judd had nothing but his tiny backpack for company. He stood for a moment, thinking someone else might appear to assist him, trying to remember the directions. When nobody appeared, he set off looking.

The instructions took him to an anonymous wooden door in a corridor full of them. He knocked softly. There was no response. Beside the frame was a small white palm reader. He held his hand out, and the door clicked open, revealing a small, plain room beyond. Single bed, bathroom, desk, wardrobe. No decoration, nothing beyond a set of blue clothes hanging in the wardrobe. He checked the labels—his size.

That confirmed it. This crap about Walker stumbling onto Judd by accident—how was it possible when they had his palm print and clothes in his size?

Closing the door behind him, he sat on the bed, staring into the mirror opposite. He looked like shit and felt completely alone. How the hell had he ended up here? He'd walked away from his life, such as it was, and for what? A room that felt a lot like a prison cell. The old man had ditched him the moment he got here.

He was alone.

He'd made a terrible mistake, he realised. He'd been beyond naive. These were telepaths. Strong ones. They'd led him here, probably planted the thought in his head. They'd known who he was, they'd lured him here.

What the hell was this place?

Chapter Two

The glide deposited Lois and Findlay ten miles outside of Atlanta at one of the city's large suburban glide ports. These were the kind where people could come and go anonymously enough, hidden in neon glows and endless shadows. Given how deep surveillance was in the cities, especially Atlanta, these were one of the few places left to go unseen. The eyes in the sky couldn't keep track of them there. As such, they'd built up as dens of crime and vice which sat uncomfortably alongside the families and business-types who were their most frequent traffic.

Lois looked like she'd come straight out of a war zone, so the first task was to sort her out before they made their separate ways back into the city. This had the added advantage of giving Lois an opportunity to find out what the hell was going on, away from prying ears and the city's network of roving digital spies, the Eyes. Findlay booked a room for a few hours at a sleazy tempotel while Lois went into the mart and printed some generic faux-wool casual wear, makeup, and bought a kit to clean her wounds.

She joined Findlay in their room after getting a dead-eyed yet somehow judgemental glare from the concierge. Her handler sat on the bed, looking like he'd rather not touch anything in the room.

'You don't mind if I change?' she asked, already peeling off what had once been quite a nice suit. Checking herself for injuries, nothing amounted to more than cuts and bruises. That was enough. She was a pretty clumsy person, but she couldn't explain away the lump swelling up above her temple. 'Findlay, what the hell am I going to do about this? How am I going to explain a black eye, a swollen cheek, and enough scrapes on my arms... Marisa will think I've been... who knows what the fuck she'll think.'

'We'll think of something,' Findlay replied, still trying to find a clean section of the bed to perch on. He was, as usual, impeccably dressed, with a suit so sharp it could cut glass. 'But I'm afraid we have more important issues at hand.'

'You've never had to hide something from Marisa,' Lois muttered under her breath, running a brush through her hair. She picked up her newly purchased makeup. 'So, what's the sitch, Findlay? Why the heavy mob? Not that I wasn't grateful.'

'Not my call,' Findlay said. 'Although I'm glad. Looked to me like the situation had gotten away from you.'

'I had it under control,' Lois lied. 'So, who ordered the extraction, and what's more important than turning the biggest slumlord in Mexico?'

'A lot's gone on while you've been south of the border,' he said, brushing some dust from his knee.

'I'm not an idiot, Findlay, I still read the feeds.'

'You know the President is on shaky ground, in terms of his poll numbers.'

'Sneaky little shit shouldn't write off ninety percent of the population.'

'Well, quite. But in order to shore up his support, he's doubled down on a lot of the subsidy games he's so fond of. Selling off parts of the national infrastructure to the megacorps for influence, control, etc. What you haven't heard is the nation's entire law enforcement infrastructure is on the market, local and federal, and there's only one player interested.'

Lois leaned on the dresser, banging her elbow against the edge as she did so, wincing and rubbing it while she took in the news. 'There's only one player big enough to make that kind of play. Sunset Industries?'

'Exactly.'

'But Sun hates the president.'

'Not for much longer, I suspect.'

'Interpol has agents inside Sunset already, so why are you pulling me out of an op three months in the making?'

'Our agent inside left a note with his handler yesterday saying he'd found something huge. This morning the bodies of both him and his handler turned up in Sweetwater Creek.'

'Here? In Atlanta?'

He nodded.

It made sense. Sunset was the largest megacorp in the world, and its headquarters were the only game in town. Everything in the city serviced it. Lois's own wife, Marisa, was a teacher at a school where over three quarters of the kids were from Sunset employees. Their own daughters fell into the other quarter.

'You're talking about Dan Sardy, right?' she asked, and everything clicked into place. She looked at her handler in horror. 'No!'

'Hear me out, Lois,' Findlay said.

'No, fuck that. The deal was always my family stays completely removed from this bullshit, Findlay. You know that.'

'For fuck's sake, Lois,' he replied, raising his voice for the first time. 'Can you hear me out?'

She sighed, put her hands on her hips and shrugged.

'We need an insider at Sunset, and quickly. You're already a resident of the city. We are not asking you to use Marisa or the girls, and we're working to find you a way in as we speak. But make no mistakes, we need you in there. We need to find out who killed our people, and why.'

'Why me? Surely the local PD are better placed.'

'You're one of our best investigators, you know corporate culture better than anyone else, and the local PD are entirely loyal to Sunset. Every single cop in there is vying to get a promotion once Sunset takes the reins. They're already talking to the local news feeds about how it was some kind of domestic situation.'

He stood, fishing out a slim pad from the inside of his jacket. He placed it on the bed and activated a cast of the crime scene files. Dan Sardy's beaten face stared blankly up at whoever had taken the photo. A deep wound snaked across his throat, halfway towards a decapitation.

Damn. Lois knew Dan, tangentially. Because he was undercover in her city, they'd been at pains to avoid each other, but they'd occasionally ended up at the same dinner parties or whatever, both enjoying being able to use their tradecraft for something so simple and meaningless. One time, at some gala dinner for teachers Marisa was up for an award at, Lois found a data clip tagged to the label inside the back of her dress when she got home. She'd booted the file to find a message which said simply 'hey there.' She hadn't even seen him at the party. But then, he was a lot better at her than this.

It hadn't been enough to save him.

'He's the first agent we've lost in over five years,' Findlay said.

'He was a good man,' she replied. 'But there're reasons behind why you and I have worked as well as we have. Never shit where you eat. This is my home, my family. If this is what could happen, you're also asking me to put my family at risk, and I can't do that.'

He placed his hands on Lois's shoulders. 'You know I wouldn't ask if we had another option here, but we need to know what's going on in that company. We need access to their files. We can get you in and out, we can protect Marisa and the girls. Hell, when this is over, we can move you wherever you like. Anywhere in the world.'

'My last mission?'

'If that's what you want. The brass need this, badly. Understand how this happened,' he said, gesturing to the flickering image of Sardy's corpse. 'Find out what was worth murdering two Interpol agents over, and we'll set you up. For life.'

Lois shook her head. Marisa talked about leaving the country all the time. Neither of them liked the way the country was going. This could be their chance.

'Fine,' she said. 'But I want it in writing. Retirement, a pension we can live on, relocation.'

'I'll get it. Go home, head back here in fourteen hours, and I'll have it, as well as a plan.'

She nodded, and stared into the dead eyes of Sardy. All she had to do was make sure she didn't end up like that.

'Two plans. One for both of us, one for Marisa if this goes to hell.'

He nodded, and left. She stood still, alone in the room with the picture of a corpse for company.

Chapter Three

The next few days on the Minos buzzed along on a cloud of caffeine and calculations, Wyn sticking to her own pod rather than mixing with the rest of the crew. If they didn't see her, they couldn't moan about her not getting enough sleep. She couldn't bring herself to go back to her bunk. When she did, she stared at the bed above, those hours the only time she felt alert and awake. Invariably, she'd be back on the flight deck within a few hours, pulling up numbers, running through entry points. If she did the prep right, she figured, it wouldn't matter how tired she was.

She kept away from the crew, except when hunger won the battle against the desire for isolation, and she had to head for the mess. That was when she couldn't avoid comments from the others.

When the Captain mandated her presence at dinner, she sat back and listened to the others, not feeling any great desire to take part. As they got closer to Europa, everyone else became increasingly animated about anything and everything except the mission itself.

When it came to politics, Wyn rarely ventured her own opinions. It wasn't that she lacked them, or couldn't argue a point, more that other people seemed so sure of their positions, their arguments, their beliefs. Back home on the feeds there were endless pontifications from the hyper-intelligent and the duller-witted alike, so entrenched in the righteous rightness of their beliefs. None seemed to accept the complexity of a world where there was rarely if ever one side to a story. So she said nothing—not out of some naiveté or lack of understanding, but because the topics of discussion were so complex she could never dream of condensing her points to the required levels of pith. She wondered why nobody else seemed to feel the same.

'No,' Barnes said, trying to keep his anger in check as he discussed the latest news on the feed of the bombing of a cafe in downtown Moscow. 'You can't lump together everyone who believes in a global redistribution of resources with these shitheads who'll bomb the shit out of innocent civilians.'

'Isn't that exactly what the west did to my people for half a century?' Hamza asked, his voice a lot calmer than the Doc's.

'You can't hold us responsible for the acts of our grandparents, either,' Barnes said. 'Shit, if we did that, we'd blame Stef for everything.'

'Hey,' Stef said, shovelling a reclaimed carbon meatball into her mouth. 'You leave my people out of this.'

'That's what Poland said,' Barnes said, a smirk spreading across his face. Stef launched her meatball in his direction.

Wyn sat, letting it wash over her. It was nice to hear people talking, at least.

She and Hamza were the only two crew members displaced from their homes by the floods. In fact, a teenaged Hamza had lived a few miles across from Wyn in London when the barriers failed. Both he and Wyn survived the floods only to be evacuated and repatriated to the lands of their ancestors. Pakistan, in his case, Nigeria, in hers. Both watched their homeland reclaimed by the sea, descending slowly into anarchy and chaos.

The other quiet one on the crew was Li Wei. Wyn had a pretty good handle on the political persuasions of the rest of the crew—even Captain Davis, himself not one to give much away. But Li, raised in China, gave nothing. Wyn had no clearer view of his opinions now than when he stepped on board four years earlier. A year or so ago Barnes and Stef made it their mission to prise something out of him, to no avail. Li had spent his life inside a regime where you didn't broadcast your opinions—a hard habit to break.

When they did get news on the feeds—time delayed and heavily censored—it still didn't paint a picture of a harmonious world. Fractious new alliances which sprang up after the floods split apart as the Mar wreaked its havoc. Stef, especially, watched her own home's descent back into madness and war with horror. Isolationism was the watchword of many nations, and though none of the crew discussed it openly, they knew there was a chance they wouldn't make it back in time even if they did work out a cure.

By the gods, Wyn was tired. Staring at the congealed bug protein on her plate, her stomach lurched. She was hungry, and tired, and she wanted nothing more than to be home again, back on her Baba's farm watching a cool Nigerian sunset.

'You okay?' Zoe asked, nudging Wyn's elbow with her own as Wyn drifted off to sleep in her chair.

'Fine,' Wyn said. 'How's mission prep coming along?'

'Same as ever. Nothing makes sense yet, certainly not the latest probe readings, but we don't have the context for them yet. Once we get on the ice, I'm hoping everything makes more sense.'

'Ladies,' Ermine said, appearing behind them stealthily enough to make Wyn jump in her chair. 'Zoe, I think the Commander should head to her bunk, don't you?'

'I...' Wyn began to protest, but the truth was she did feel tired. Not just tired, though. This was different. Groggy. What had Zoe just said? It seemed to slip off the surface of her brain. Her eyes felt heavy, and she nodded. Maybe she could sleep. 'I should go,' she said, trying to stand, but the words slurred. Her legs felt disembodied, like they belonged to someone else.

This was wrong. Something was wrong.

'Let me help you,' Zoe said. She slipped an arm around Wyn's waist. 'Come on,' she said, and led her out of the mess.

'Something... wrong,' Wyn slurred. Her head lolled about like her neck couldn't hold it up.

'You're fine,' Zoe said. 'Just need some sleep.' She eased Wyn into her bunk, where the mattress above her swirled. Everything blurred. Someone pulled her boots off, and a sense of calm washed over her. She was dimly aware of a sheet pulled up to cover her, the curtain closing, before exhaustion won through.

Chapter Four

The commute in from the outskirts of the city meant a ride on the city's closed-loop system. Atlanta had been one of the first cities to ban personal transportation, meaning the only way you could get anywhere was on the loop, or by foot. There were private carriers down in certain parts of the city run by local gangs, criminals who used them to transport illicit goods around the city. You get busted by local PD in one of those, you could be damn sure you'd get tagged as trafficking in whatever your driver was. For Lois, the risk was too great, no matter how much quicker the pods got about the place.

Leaning her head against the window, she took in the city. From the outside it looked majestic—one of the few urban centres in America which hadn't fallen into decay, or fallen to the tides. In reality, Atlanta was a law unto itself, and the law was Sunset.

Possibly the largest megacorp on the globe at this point, Sunset remained under the sole ownership of Christopher Sun—a man so enigmatic there were more rumours and speculation printed about him every day than there were pads to read it on. His father, another Christopher, formed a pharma company over a hundred years earlier, and had used its rapid growth to accumulate power in a way that would become the blueprint for the other megacorps. Sun himself was simultaneously one of the most famous yet least visible people on the planet.

Sunset had started a few miles outside the city, but soon took over what had once been a thriving, diverse city, turning it into one giant headquarters. Those headquarters themselves dominated the skyline, huge spires of glass and steel reaching almost to the clouds. Smaller towers spread out in a circle around, tiny suckerfish clinging desperately to the side of the shark. These buildings held the subsidiary companies, the support network. The rest of the city ran entirely to maintain this behemoth at its centre, and took on most of its aesthetic, too. Gleaming metal and vast expanses of glass were the order of things, with little left of the city it had once been. It was modern, thriving, and entirely and corporately bland.

Still, it was the safest city in the country, which was why she and Marisa had moved here five years earlier. Once it became clear Lois's job would have her away for months at a time, they decided to move somewhere safe, quiet, and with decent jobs, so she wouldn't have to worry about her family. Look how that was panning out.

The closer she got to the residential district of Westview she called home, the more the knot in her stomach grew. She was going to have to tell Marisa. It would not be a comfortable conversation. Usually, this trip back home was a joyous occasion, with her girls waiting to meet her at the station. Not today.

The link pulled into Westview. Lois stood, catching a look at herself in the mirror. The swelling on her face hadn't gone anywhere, nor the cut on her lip. The clothes she'd hurriedly purchased looked baggy, ill-fitting. She looked tired, broken. She felt that way, too.

Her apartment was a few blocks away, so she walked in failing evening light through pristine streets, past pristine people—some of whom gave the slow-shuffling woman a wide berth. Every step seemed to build the pressure in her chest.

By the time she reached the house she was a bundle of nerves. She could have scanned herself in, but decided it was better to knock.

'Mommy!' Her two girls saw her through the viewer, the door burst open, and two sets of bouncing brown curls bounded through the door, the children attached to them slamming into her in a wave of cuddles.

'Hey girls.' She drank in the smell of them, the touch of them, the essence of them, drawing strength with every second of contact. 'Did you have a good day? Where's Mama?'

'She's in a bad mood,' Stacey replied, pouting.

'Oh dear,' Lois said.

'Mommy,' Rosa said, pulling her face away and looking at her mother for the first time. 'What happened to your face?'

'Oh, nothing,' Lois lied, reluctantly letting go of her babies. Each took a hand, guiding her through to the kitchen. The smell of paprika couldn't mask the tang of burnt food.

'Who is it, girls?' Marisa called back, her attention on the stove. Food and pans covered every surface.

'Hey, Mama,' Lois said, leaning as nonchalantly as she could in the doorframe, peering around the corner.

Marisa whirled round with a start. Her dark hair was up, and she wore sweat pants and a tank top, its front dusted liberally in flour. She looked stunning, even so.

'Lois?' Marisa said. She dropped her ladle and bounded across to Lois, planting a heavy kiss on her wife. Lois's arms went around her neck, and she drank in the smell of the love of her life.

Marisa did the exact same as Rosa, pulling away after the elation had dissipated, taking stock of the bedraggled woman in front of her. 'What the hell happened?'

'I'll tell you later,' Lois replied. 'Can I enjoy being home for a minute?'

Marisa nodded, not satisfied, but not pressing it either. She laughed. 'Well, you picked a hell of a time. I've completely fucked up dinner.'

'Mama!' the two girls shouted in unison.

'Nonsense,' Lois said, pulling away. Marisa always dealt with stress by working it out in the kitchen, but given she found the kitchen to be the most stressful place in the world, Lois never understood why. 'Let me try.'

Marisa fetched a ladle, scooping up a ladle of broth.

Lois took a sip. It was vaguely burned, but hardly ruined. 'Stick it in another pan.'

'Do you see any other pans?' Marisa sighed, and tipped the whole lot into the sink, where the reclaimators set to work on it, sifting out the salvageable carbon for re-use. Their food for the next few days would taste slightly burned. 'Fuck it, we'll order in. We should celebrate, anyway.'

'How are you doing?'

'Urgh, the two monsters have been driving me insane. I can't wait for them to go back to school. I barely got any work done. I'm way behind on my lesson prep.' She sighed. 'It's not their fault. They're bored. There's nothing for them to do. They can't even go and play in the park because of these stupid new bylaws. I mean, in Pittsburgh there were kids out in the street during the holidays, but look outside. You'd think this was a city without children.'

She was right. They'd come here to keep up with Lois's ever changing circumstances, and because it seemed like a safe place to raise kids. It turned out to be safe in the way hermetically-sealed vegetables are safe. But where in the hell else could they go that would be as safe?

Getting through this one job and getting the hell away from America was the way to go. They could move to the Bahamas, or Eastern Europe. Anywhere but here. The idea seemed, for the first time, achievable.

'So,' Marisa said, washing her hands and throwing the towel on top of the general kitchen clutter. 'Are you going to tell me why you look like complete shit and are home three weeks early?'

Lois took a deep breath, trying to work out exactly how much to tell her wife. 'Sure,' she said. 'Let's order dinner first.'

Chapter Five

Wyn awoke in total darkness. The inside of her mouth felt glued shut. Forcing her dry tongue around it, it stuck to the roof, shutting off her supply of air for a second. Panicking, she coughed, sat up, and smacked her head off the bunk above. With a moan of pain she groped for the curtain, scrabbling to pull it across.

'Uh...fff...' she said, to nobody. She tried to focus her bleary eyes. 'Miles?' she said, but the sound escaping her throat sounded nothing like it.

'Yes, Commander?'

'What time is it?'

'Oh-eight-hundred and fifteen minutes.'

Not so bad. She might have finally had a decent night's sleep. 'Status?'

The other bunks were empty, beds made, curtains open. She could see the dog-eared book on Stef's pillow, its cover in German. She tried to focus on the lettering, but it danced out of her comprehension.

'Ship is operating under normal parameters,' Miles replied.

She put her feet on the floor, and an arm out to steady herself. 'Distance to manoeuvre?'

'Well...'

'Miles?'

'You should get up.'

Pulling on some fresh clothes, she got to her feet unsteadily and pulled her boots back on. Her hands shot out as she stepped forward, steadying herself against the sensation of everything swimming, and the bile rising in her empty stomach. 'What the fuck is going on, Miles?'

'The XO decided you needed rest ahead of the final approach to Europa, so he administered you an ambi.'

'He did what?' she said, stomach churning again as she raised her voice. 'How long until we enter the bracket?'

'I was about to wake you, anyway...'

'How long, Miles?'

'You've missed some developments. You should go and see the Captain.'

She shook her head. 'Ermine. Motherfucker. Wait until I get my hands on him.'

'Commander.'

She stopped, and sighed. 'I know. Calm down, right?'

'The XO is thinking about ship security. Which is his job.'

'Still, fuck him with a rusty hook. How dare he give me a med without my permission? He could have asked me to go to bed.'

She sighed again.

'Okay, fine, he did ask me. Whatever. I need coffee.'

'If you go and see Doctor Barnes, he might be able to provide you with something to refresh yourself.'

'Barnes, right. Yeah, I'd like a word with him, too.'

The light outside the bunks was achingly bright, and took away what small sense of equilibrium she'd clawed back. Heading through to the mess, the whole crew were there, eating their breakfasts. Her stomach turned. She might be hungry, but couldn't face the prospect of bacon formed from crushed beetle hinds.

As she appeared in the doorway, the crew stopped and turned to face her as one. Some stood, unsure how to react. One look at their faces and she knew —they were all in on it. She ignored them, walking around the outside of the mess and on to the med bay, where Barnes sat at his desk, staring through a viewer at some samples.

'You drugged me,' she barked.

He bolted up in his chair. 'I...'

'Do it again without asking me first, and I'll take one of your scalpels and cut your bollocks off, okay?'

'I...'

'You've said that already.'

'I didn't want to... I had orders.'

'Always a rock solid defence.'

'Wyn, please,' he said, rising from his seat.

'I need to get sharp,' she said, cutting off his apology. 'I've no idea what's going on and I'm going to have to do several day's work in one day.'

'I could give you a stim?'

'Well, ordinarily I'd tell you stims are a terrible idea when you have to do computational analysis, because they lead to increased margins of error and false confidence in your abilities but fuck it, I guess I don't have a choice.' She glared at him and rolled up her sleeve, holding her forearm out defiantly.

He opened a drawer, taking out a small vial of clear liquid and an injector. He loaded the shot up, pressed the end to her wrist, and administered the injection. The hiss of the tiny gun echoed in pain up her arm as the drug pumped into her bloodstream.

Barnes opened his mouth to say something further, but Wyn had already rolled her sleeve down and turned her back on him.

Ignoring the mess once more, she strode to the pilot's module. The hatch stood open, which she knew meant one thing. Sure enough, Ermine waited inside the cramped module. At least he had the good grace to sit in the co-pilot chair. She walked past him and strapped herself in.

'You have something to say to me, Commander?' Ermine asked in a cool but somewhat adversarial tone.

'No.'

'Good,' he said, though Wyn enjoyed the note of disappointment in his voice. He got out of his chair, and turned to leave.

'I'm quite capable of looking after myself,' she said, instantly regretting rising to the bait.

'It's funny,' he replied, turning back. 'I don't recall much evidence of that. Oh, and there's been some changes while you've been asleep. Might want to look into them.'

She sat in her seat, staring forward, seething. She didn't even notice him leaving, too busy trying to come up with a witty retort.

Reaching forward, she booted up the screens. Consoles flashed with diagnostics. She stared at them, still seething. How dare he drug her, without consent? He must have dosed her food, with Barnes's help. And the rest of the crew must have been in on it, too. Was the Captain? What if the order actually came from him? Zoe had carried her to her bunk, had she known?

Shaking her head, she stared at the screens until the rage subsided and she could focus on what they said.

They said something strange.

'Miles?'

'Yes, Commander?'

'What's this approach vector?'

'There's been an amendment to the flight plan and landing profile.'

'What?'

'I'm sorry. I wanted to inform you, but it's been a bit rushed since you woke up. I did try and tell you there's been some developments.'

'What the fuck's happened, Miles?'

'You've been asleep for three full cycles. Yesterday, we received word from Sunset. They have developed a more optimal approach vector.'

'So how long until we make our final approach?'

'Forty-seven hours.'

'What? No. There's no fucking way.'

'I've checked the numbers. They are sound. The new approach gets us on an earlier slingshot and to Europa six days early.'

She frowned at the numbers on screen. 'I did these calculations. I discussed them with the Captain. We decided the risks were too high. For one thing the slingshot comes in damn hot. It'll put a lot of pressure on the Minos, and on me if I can't control the G Forces. And it brings us onto the surface at the tail end of a magnetotail window. They'll not have long to get us under the ice.'

'According to the mission calculations, there will be a seven-hour window for drilling. Sunset puts the chances of success at over eighty percent.'

'So, there's a twenty percent chance we get cooked in our suits? Doesn't exactly fill me with confidence. The Captain approved this?'

'I assume so. It was Ermine who inputted the changes.'

She shook her head. Something about this seemed weird.

'Miles, open my exonet feed.' The official ISS communications feed opened in a separate portal. A handful of new messages from the past three days, including one from her father, but there was no order to change the approach vector. Nothing from them, in fact, which would make it the first time since they left

Earth they'd gone three whole days without pestering her. No official comms.

'Change it back,' she said. 'I've not had a direct order to change it, and I'm not sending everyone down to the surface with a one in five shot of getting cooked before they can even start. They're not prepped for this.' She got up from her chair. 'Recalculate the entry.'

'Where are you going?'

'I need to tell the Captain his XO has gone rogue. Drugging me. Changing flight plans. We can still undo this.'

'But...'

'What?'

'I can't change it.'

'Why not?'

'The XO outranks you.'

She sighed. 'Wait here.'

'I can't wait here,' he replied. 'I'm incorporeal.'

Ignoring him, she strode out of the pod.

Chapter Six

The pizzas in this town were as depressing as in Tijuana. Still, after an hour of bathing the kids, reading them stories, giving them cuddles she wanted to last forever, and looking through the mail built up over the last few months, Lois was at last sat with a glass of wine and a slice of something that bore no relation to either bread or cheese.

'This tastes even worse than my meal,' Marisa said, mouth half full. She put her plate down on the table next to Lois's, and picked up her own glass. She stared at Lois. This was the first thing she'd said since Lois had gone into detail about Tijuana and the subsequent meeting with Findlay.

'We could move somewhere where they still have real food, once this is over,' Lois said.

Marisa arched her eyebrow. 'That's if any of us survive.' She stared at her feet, rubbing the arches, absently, before turning her attention back to Lois. 'The whole point of this job was to get in and out without anyone knowing who you are. I always accepted there was a level of risk in what you did, but I thought your handlers were supposed to keep you away from the sharp end of things?'

'They never planned for this. The way it went in Mexico was my fault as much as anyone else. I got too close to it. I wanted to be the one to take that slippery fucker down, not leave it to someone else. I wanted him to know. Childish.'

Marisa shook her head. 'Tijuana. Jesus. I thought you were in Canada. You could at least have popped in to see my family while you were down there.'

Lois laughed. 'I think I'd rather have ended up at gunpoint.'

Marisa smiled, but it faded quickly. 'I can't lose you, Lois. I can't do this on my own, you know that, right? When you first took this job, it was going to be for a few years, then you'd get a transfer into a desk job somewhere.'

'I know.'

'I mean, look at your face. Now you want to walk into the lion's mouth, when there's already dead agents? In this city?'

'I know,' Lois added. She wished there was a strong counter-argument, but there wasn't.

They sat in silence together, listening to the inane chatter of their girls, completely oblivious as they sat in their bedroom making up stories for each other.

'Do you owe it to this person?' Marisa asked. 'The murdered agent?'

'Kind of. That's a part of it. If the same happened to me wouldn't you want someone looking?'

'And you want to do this?'

'Yes? No? I don't know. I don't think I have a choice. I don't want to do anything that puts you at risk. Maybe you and the girls get out of town for a few weeks? You could go to my Mom's?

'No. The point of choosing you is your local roots. We're your in. How's it going to look if we up sticks and disappear?'

'I don't care, if it means you'll be safe,' she said, voice louder than she'd intended. She cast a look to the bedroom door to make sure the girls weren't listening. It had gone quiet through there.

'Well, I do care if it makes you less safe. You said it yourself, we get through this, it's our golden ticket. We focus on that. Any sign of trouble, we split. All of us. Interpol be damned.'

Lois nodded, and looked her wife in the eyes. Tears sprang to her own, unbidden. 'I love you,' she said.

'Right back at you,' Marisa said, smiling. 'Besides, it'll be kind of novel having you around, helping out. You can take the girls into school some days.'

'I'd love to.'

'I hate this place, Lois. I don't think it's healthy for the girls. It's like a cult. You should see their homework. *Write a paper on Sunset and how it has a positive impact on the world around you.* And the people around here, they're so corporate and weird. The other day, Cyndi popped round, completely unannounced. Said Billy missed the girls, and could they come in. I told her I was sorry, but I was working. She looked completely shocked. Had no idea I worked. Half an hour it took me to get rid of her, most of which was me trying to explain the basic concept of a non-Sunset job.'

'Well, you start thinking about where you want us to go.'

Marisa took a deep swig of her wine, and reached forward to her pizza again. She stopped, mid-bite, and threw the slice back down in disgust. 'This is grim,' she said, the half-chewed pizza still in her mouth.

'Yeah, let's not go there again.'

'You can call it reclaimed carbon all you like. Still tastes of bugs.'

Lois didn't say anything. Marisa took another swig of wine, and they sat in silence for a moment, Lois deep in thought about what awaited tomorrow.

'You having second thoughts?' Marisa asked, poking Lois in the stomach with her big toe.

'What? No,' Lois said. 'Yes. I don't know. Thinking.'

'Well,' Marisa said, putting her glass down. 'We've both done enough of that for one day. Let's try something else.' She leaned forward, running her hand gently through Lois's blonde curls, and pulled her forward. Her lips were still wet with wine.

'Are the kids asleep?' Lois asked.

Marisa leaned back and poked her head around the corner. She looked back, nodding her head and biting her bottom lip. Lois swung her legs out and stood, helping Marisa up. They kissed once more, their bodies pressing into one another, before Lois let herself be led to the bedroom.

Chapter Seven

For hours, Judd alternated between stewing, sitting, pacing, and staring at the walls. The room had no windows, and he'd left his pad back on the Key, so the bare walls were the only place to look. He ran through his memories of the previous night again and again, trying to work out if his thoughts had been his own, whether they'd drugged him. Both impossible to know, but the choices he'd made, they somehow didn't feel... his.

He tried to focus on hearing the thoughts of others in the building, but he'd never been able to anywhere else, so it failed, somewhat predictably. What if he didn't even have the gift? What if it had been Walker projecting into him?

He went back to pacing, then picked through the package left for him. Blue uniform, a wash kit, no pad. No viewer in the room, no connection to the outside world. He was completely cut off.

This was a parallel world, one inhabited by people he'd spent his life in fear and hate of. Never mind that he was one of them, he felt no connection to their cause. He'd had a half decent chat with one old man and walked away from his whole life.

Another hour of waiting. He wondered if anyone had noticed his absence back home yet. He had a semi-decent social life on the feeds, but it'd be days there before anyone noticed he hadn't posted. If at all. Work had probably already replaced him, and his roommate would be so stoned he'd not notice Judd's absence for days. The only people who might give the remotest shit about his sudden absence would be the poor bastards tasked with replacing him on his shifts.

There was a gentle knock on the door. Judd span round as the door slid open. He expected Walker, but a woman stood in the hallway, dressed in the blue uniform. She looked Chinese, perhaps, with a bob framing a quizzical look on her face. She was also cute, with a smirk that seemed to sit permanently below a button nose.

'Not changed?'

'Sorry?'

'Not a problem. Come with me.'

She turned and abruptly headed back into the corridor.

'Wait,' he said, following her. 'I'm not sure what's going on. I'd like to talk to Walker, straighten this out.'

She laughed, looking back with that gorgeous smile on her face. 'You think we've abducted you, right? Standard response. It all happens so quickly. You want out, you're free to go, but I wouldn't advise running out into the moors. You never know what's out there.' She laughed again, but saw Judd wasn't joining her in her mirth. She stopped, allowing Judd to catch up. 'Look, Mr Walker is a busy man, but he asked me personally to show you around. I can answer questions you might have, or find someone who can. But it's getting late, and there're no glides out of here until tomorrow.'

'I...' Judd stammered, wanting both to argue with her and kick up a fuss, and also to impress her and woo her in some way he didn't quite know how to manage.

She turned and headed off down the corridor. 'I'm Lan,' she called back. 'You're Judd, right?' Her manner was so bright and breezily out of keeping with his own mood.

He nodded and tried to keep up.

'Let's go to the canteen, get you some food. You hungry?'

'Sure.'

'Man, I've always wanted to go to the moon. You'll have to tell me about it.'

He mumbled something vaguely affirmative, while trying to place her accent. She sounded English, but not quite at the same time.

She led him into a wide, cavernous dining room, empty for the most part. Long tables ran along the room, with a canteen at the far end. Bigger even than the canteen at the Key, Judd guessed this could hold a few hundred people comfortably. A handful of people milled about, none of whom paid attention to the new arrivals.

Lan motioned to a bench. 'Can I get you a drink?'

'Sure, whatever they have.'

She bounded away, her bubbliness entirely at odds with his growing unease. He didn't trust her, or any of this. He stared at the table, trying to keep his thoughts under control, until she came back and placed a clear bottle in front of him.

'This stuff is lovely. It's basically water, but chemically altered to taste like pure fruit juice. I swear, you can't even taste the difference.'

He nodded his thanks and took a sip. Summer fruits flooded his mouth, so intense they made his eyes water. He spluttered.

'Sorry,' she said. 'It can be a bit much at first.'

'It's fine,' he said, waving away her concern and trying to appear heroically stoic. What the hell for? This wasn't a date, for Christ's sake. She could be his enemy.

She smiled. 'So, Judd. I guess you're probably wondering what the hell is going on, right?'

'You could say that.'

'Well, let me start by saying we all wish Mr Walker wasn't the one doing community outreach for us. He's not a people person. He hooks people in, that's for sure, but he's got so much going on running this place, people end up coming here confused and thinking they've made a mistake.'

'Have I?'

'God, no. Trust me, you're going to love it here. I notice we're conversing externally?'

He wasn't sure what she meant, and must have shown it on his face, because the smile came back. Not condescending, but not far off.

'Talking. We're not inside our heads. So you've got the gift, but you don't use it?'

'You're a teep, too?'

The smile disappeared for a second, coming back at half-force. 'I don't like that word, but yes. I have the gift. Like you, I spent most of my life hiding it, until I met Mr Walker. I came here, learned how to use it. Now I can do things I would never have believed possible.'

Judd's face flushed. The thought of this woman peeking inside his mind made his stomach lurch. She didn't seem to be reading his mind, but even if she did, would he know?

'Like what?' he asked.

'Well...' She placed her hand on the table and moved her fingers in a kind of wave. The bottle inched toward her.

Judd almost fell off his bench. 'Holy shit. I didn't even know that was possible. Can I do that?'

She laughed. 'We won't know until we run some tests, train you up, but it's possible. The Tk gene is related to the Tp gene, and most Tk's are also Tp, but it's not so often in the other direction.'

'What else?'

'Other gifts? Just the two, but with infinite shades and variations. We're talking about less than one percent of less than one percent of the world's population. It's not like this is a latent part of people's brains. As far as we know, everyone with the gene presents at some point in their lives. But the exciting part is, even with everything we can do so far, the labs think we're only using a fraction of what's available to us. So there could be more powers than two, around the corner. But with such a small pool to choose from, we don't have a big enough sample size to judge. Hungry?'

'I, uh...'

She motioned to a man not in uniform, who scurried over. 'Can we get some omelettes?'

He scurried away.

'What are the labs?' Judd asked. 'What is this place?'

She frowned again, but given the way it crinkled the top of her nose, he didn't entirely mind. 'Walker didn't tell you much, did he? I swear he's getting worse. I mean, I know he's old, but... This is Psy-Ops. Or at least, that's what we call it. It doesn't have an official name. It's a research facility to understand more about psychometry, telepathy, telekinesis, but to most of us it's just... home. To those of us who choose to train here, and those who choose to remain here outside the glare of mainstream society.'

'A home for the gifted?'

'Exactly.' She leaned across the table. 'It's more than that, obviously. It's also a defence against those who would choose to use us for ill, or want to eradicate us.'

'A haven?'

'Something like that.'

The little man hurried back over with two plates, each of which contained fluffy, yellow omelettes, served with a small sprinkling of chips. He placed them down, gave a little bow, and scurried off again.

'Wait,' Judd said, leaning over his plate. 'Are these real?'

'Mmmhmm,' Lan replied through a mouthful of real eggs. 'The farms around here are certified as a hundred percent Mar-free.'

Judd looked back toward the little man who'd returned to the kitchen. 'What about them?' Judd asked.

'Who?'

'Farmers. Chefs. Support staff. Do they know what goes on here?'

'Some. Most of them who do, don't care. Floods decimated this part of the country. Whitby, the town itself, is completely gone. There's still a bit of the old Abbey sticking out of the water, but only the high farmlands and the villages around survived. After came the disease. An entire area cut off from the rest of the country. The consortium funding this place came in and funded a complete restoration. We brought the farmlands back from the brink. Built a hospital to deal with the sickness, and built this place, which has its own thriving economy around it. The villages within ten miles of here are in a better state than before the floods. Fewplaces in England can say that.'

'Yeah, but...' he leaned across the table. 'Don't you worry they could be, I dunno, spies?'

She smirked once more. 'Once you've been here a while, you'll understand things better.'

He took another bite of eggs. 'What if I want to leave?'

'Be a shame, but we're not holding you here. There's a glide tomorrow. I can't say we'll pay for transport back to the moon, but we can get you back to Paris, if that's what you want.'

'Nobody is going to come after me?'

'Come after you for what?'

'For what I know.'

She laughed, covering her mouth so as not to spray him with omelette. 'Dude, who would you tell? Do you think the governments of the world don't know we're here? We have an old radar listening base about thirty miles away from here, which is probably listening to this conversation, even as we speak. This place isn't secret, but it's ours. Let me ask you a question.'

'Go on,' he said, trying not to feel humiliated by her mocking laughter.

'You've lived your entire life with this secret, right? Aren't you the least bit curious what your gift could actually be? What you could do with it?'

He leaned back. 'I spent most of my life trying not to think about it. Once I decided not to tell anyone, not even my parents, I shut that part of me away and got as far away as I could from anyone who might suspect. I still have no idea how you lot even knew to look for me.'

'We have our ways.'

He sighed. 'Is there a part of me who wants to go down this rabbit hole? Sure. But I'm scared. Of you. Of every other person in a blue uniform—FYI, not the most comforting of looks—I never looked into what my life as a tee... as someone with a gift... might be, because I didn't want to know. I didn't want it, for me, or for anyone around me. This... gift... nothing scares me more.'

She leaned back in her chair and appraised him, coldly. There was still a hint of the playfulness there, around the edge of her mouth.

'Look,' Judd said, pushing the empty plate forward and standing up awkwardly from the table, 'I should get that glide. Go back to my job, hope they've not given it to someone else.'

'Sure.' She stood, too. 'I'll need to take you back to your room until we can arrange it. You'll need to stick around until tomorrow.'

He shrugged. 'Okay.'

'Please don't leave your room. This place isn't a secret, but there are secrets here, so...'

'I understand.'

She walked him back along the corridor without further discussion until they came back to his room. He held his palm to the pad, and the door slid open.

'Could I get a pad, or something to keep me occupied while I wait?'

'I'll see what I can do,' she replied, more curtly than she'd spoken before. 'It was nice meeting you.'

'You too, and hey, I'm sorry.'

'No skin off my nose. Good luck, Judd.'

She turned, and the door slid shut once more.

Judd sat on the bed, staring at the bare walls once more. The room's silence felt more oppressive, and soon he was up and pacing about, staring at the door, willing it to open.

There was no pad coming.

They must have had a reason to fly him here. They wouldn't do all that just to let him leave, surely? And what secrets was she talking about?

He lay on the bed, staring at the white ceiling, listening to people pass up and down the corridor, their voices distant.

He should try to find out more, without a chaperone this time. Try to work out why the hell the head of a secret organisation of telepaths would fly to the moon for some random kid. Get a proper sense of what he was dealing with. If he could find some kind of evidence to go with this gnawing feeling in his gut, he'd feel a lot better getting on that glide tomorrow.

'Fuck it,' he said, finally, and opened the door, heading out into the corridor.

Chapter Eight

Back at the glide centre, Lois headed back to the same hotel, taking up residence at the bar. She knew which room to meet Findlay in, but wanted to do a bit of reconnaissance before picking up the key. She picked up a disposable pad, a single pane of glass upon which pre-programmed news feeds scrolled in pre-packaged bites. The ultimate in sanitised news. Still, people got them each day, happy to have news fitting their world view.

Lois stared through the type to the lobby, tracking the comings and goings of the patrons. A family looking exhausted; two businessmen heading up for an illicit affair; a hooker trying to entice a rotund man to her room. She watched the family, a couple and two boys, the latter running around with kid versions of Oc's, playing some kind of laser tag with each other that turned the world into a battlefield. Every now and again the father would attempt to stop them, but his heart wasn't in it. The mother ignored them, probably the wiser move.

After half an hour, satisfied nothing was untoward and there wasn't direct surveillance of the hotel, she went to the front desk. She picked up her key and wandered over to the lifts. She rode to the top floor, crossed to the other set of lifts and took another back down to the fifth, where she found Findlay coming the other way. They met at the door and went inside.

Findlay immediately set about scanning the room for surveillance. The two of them stayed silent, Lois pulling up a chair and easing her feet out of her shoes. She rubbed the soles, which had ached for days.

'Done,' Findlay said. 'How are you?'

'My feet hurt.'

'If that's the only problem, I'd say you're not doing too bad.'

'Touché. How are you?'

He blew out a lungful of air exaggeratedly. 'It's been a busy day. How the hell did you get such a delightful house in this city? I've ended up with a hole with damp walls that's right next to the loop. My bed shakes every seventeen and a half minutes.'

'They like to have their teachers close to the schools, and Marisa's very good at her job,' she said.

'I need a Marisa,' Findlay said.

'You can't have mine.'

He smiled an endearing smile, before grabbing a chair and sitting opposite. 'What did you tell her?'

'The truth.'

He took this in for a moment. 'How much of the truth?'

'Everything. I don't have secrets from my wife, and if she's going to back me in this, she needs to know the full extent of the risks.'

'And?'

'Absolutely delighted, as you can imagine.'

'Is she in?'

'As long as you come through on your promises.'

Findlay opened his bag and pulled out a pad. Interpol issue—a secure briefing docket, a standalone item that couldn't connect to the feeds. He handed it to Lois, who placed her thumb on the glass, waking the device. She scanned the contract that came up on the screen. It released her from her obligation, gave a severance figure that was more than generous, a relocation package, and confirmed a final pension. There was even a life insurance policy attached which doubled her current one, in the event she died in the line of duty.

'This seems pretty decent,' she said.

'Keep reading,' he said. 'The stuff you won't like is on page four.'

She scanned further. 'What the fuck?'

'They were adamant.'

'If I bring down the biggest megacorp on the planet I get a nice payout, but if I fail I get nothing?'

'The life insurance pays out if you die trying, and I promise you I'd get Marisa and the girls out. But yes. They're desperate. They need a win here. The word on the grapevine is every single multinational agency, from Interpol to IMF to UN, is running scared of the power Christopher Sun has.'

'Not so scared they'll do right by me if I can't find anything?'

He shrugged. Lois could tell by his face this was as good as it got, that he'd run out of options, too. She trusted that he'd gone to bat for her as best he could.

'Say I turn this assignment down. What then?'

'Are you planning on it?'

'What are they going to do?'

He sighed. 'Absolutely nothing. But...' He pulled his pad out and called up the image of Coyne. The word Deceased ran underneath the picture. 'Coyne's people are regrouping. It seems the cartels are more than a little pissed the man washing their money has turned up dead. So far, they're focusing their ire on the local PD, but there's already been a few attempts to hack into the local network to see who is actually responsible. Obviously as an Interpol agent you're protected, but if you walk away, some of that protection disappears.'

Heat rising up her neck, Lois turned on her handler. 'Excuse me? Interpol is going to... *blackmail me?*'

'No, Lois, but you have to look at this objectively.'

'It's not Interpol, objectively, who's putting their life on the line. Again. And bringing my family into the firing line.'

'I understand...'

'You don't understand shit.'

'Don't I?' he shouted, the first time Lois could remember him doing so. It was enough to snap her out of her anger for a second.

'I don't think you do, no,' she replied, although by the fire in his eyes she'd misjudged that.

He shook his head. 'Do you think you're the only agent I'm handler for? I've got seven other agents. I have to ask every one of them to risk their lives, and I risk my own every time I go to meet one of them. I've got a family too, you know? You don't even know about them, and there's a damn good reason, because if one of you got tortured, I wouldn't want to worry about you turning on me when I should focus on rescuing you. That's not to mention...' he tapped the pad, bringing up the images of Sardy's death scene. 'You asked about Sardy, how he died, but he didn't die alone. His handler's image is right here, and you never even commented on it. Oh, and I've got to take on three of her agents on, in the middle of a crisis.' He sighed. 'I'm sorry,' he said, letting the anger dissipate. 'I know this is bad. It's fucked up. But we are where we are.'

They stood for a moment, facing each other. Finally, Lois crossed the gap between them, and pulled Findlay into a hug. He returned it, tightly. As they pulled away, Findlay brushed the corner of his eye with his sleeve.

'Okay then,' Lois said. 'Let's get to work.'

Chapter Nine

He should have put the uniform on. If sneaking around a secret facility filled with people who could crawl into his brain to find out secrets was the plan, blending in would be a good start. But Judd was already in the corridor; going back seemed like giving up.

Adopting the most nonchalant walk he could, he walked back toward the front entrance. He'd seen the canteen, and there hadn't been much along that corridor. People passed him without a care, and he tried to keep his thoughts ordered, calm. He still had no idea how this teep bullshit worked and didn't want to go round broadcasting his intention to every bluecoat he passed.

He turned the corner into the atrium, coming face to face with around twenty uniformed men and women, each of whom looked up in unison. He gave a little grimace he hoped would translate into a normal facial expression and walked toward them. As one, they looked away, going back about their business. They looked to be heading through a series of barriers leading deeper into the building, so he fell in behind them, hoping they'd sweep him up in their number and propel him deeper inside.

As a plan, it worked brilliantly—right until they came to the scanners. Those at the front of the group waved their palms at the gates, and they swooshed open long enough for one individual to go through, before closing behind them. Shit. There was no way he'd be able to follow one of them out. He doubted waving his own hand would do the job, either.

He could jump the barrier. Sure, the three burly guards on the far side would probably beat him to death before he hit the ground, but he'd be on the other side.

The crowd moved through, and he was out of ideas. Maybe…

'Judd?'

He whirled round to see Lan, her face confused.

'What are you doing?'

'Um…'

'I said you were free to go. Next glide isn't until tomorrow morning. What were you going to do? Run across the moors?'

He shrugged. Did she think he was escaping? Better that than his actual intentions, he supposed.

'I could take you outside now. Forecast is about minus four tonight, so you're going to die of hypothermia out there, but if you're that desperate to go I could get my coat? You're heading the wrong direction though, FYI.'

Judd looked at his shoes. Was this going to end up with him walking the moors on his own? His loafers weren't ideal hill walking equipment. 'No, I'll stay.'

'Good. As long as you're here, I could show you a bit more of what we do here?'

'Sure,' he said. Heart pounding, he gave her as sincere a smile as he could muster. He'd gotten away with it. Or had he? Lan could almost certainly read his mind, see his true intent. Was she protecting him from the beating he'd catch for spying?

Others around him had taken in their conversation. Judd's cheeks went red. He wanted to go back to his room and wait for the ground to swallow him whole, but playing it cool seemed the better option. Besides, if it was a choice between a few hours with Lan and a few hours staring at the walls, he might as well have the company. He might even find what he was looking for.

'Come on.' Scanning him through, she led him down a different corridor. Each door had a glass screen to see through. Inside were classrooms full of people staring forward or at each other, sitting silently.

'People work this late at night?' Judd asked.

'Not working. Learning. Once you get more understanding about your power, chances are you'll work night and day to learn more. It might not be much to look at, but in these classrooms, people are learning to use their talents in different ways. In this room, students are learning to repel an attack from a fellow gifted. Likewise, the people opposite are learning to probe past their defences. It's done under controlled circumstances, with a mediator monitoring both sides to ensure nothing goes wrong.'

He peered through the window. People sat in groups of three, staring at each other in silence.

'Why don't you try to listen in?' Lan said.

'What?'

'Reach out with your mind. See if you can work out what they're pushing.'

'I... I have no idea how to do that.'

She smiled and put her hand on his shoulder. 'It's not a trick. Try. Worst that'll can happen is you won't hear anything. Clear your mind and focus.'

Frowning, he looked back through the window, reaching out. He didn't know what he was doing, but he tried to listen. The noise in his head increased until there were three voices. He closed his eyes and tried to focus, to distinguish words in the whisper.

'January. February. March. One of them is reciting months of the year.'

'Good. Anything else?'

He tried to block out the months, and focused on the other voice. Except...

'It's not words, it's... a vase. A blue vase.'

She squeezed his shoulder, and a tremor of excitement ran down his spine. 'Good,' she said. 'You saw the attack, and the defence. If you're trying to read someone's mind and there's no way in, quite often an image will be more useful than trying to dig through. Suggesting an image tied to a memory will cause the memory to surface, and break the pattern the defender is trying to use to block you out. That's why the other person recited months, trying to create a pattern, a shield if you like, to deflect the efforts of the other. Who do you think is winning?'

'The defender. The other guy wasn't getting anywhere with his image.'

'Good. You've got promise. Took me a good few attempts to listen in. Come on, let's go see something more exciting.'

They carried on, twisting and turning through more corridors, each lined with classrooms until they passed through a heavy door into a separate part of the building. Here the rooms were the size of gymnasiums. On the left, combat training, while on the other side of the corridor four uniformed kids stood in a line. Across from them sat a range of objects.

'Here we go,' Lan said. 'This should be interesting.'

At one end of the room a man stood on a dais, whistle in hand. He raised it to his lips and blew. Each student changed their stance, raising their hands. Objects arranged in a row across from them raised up, floating a foot from the floor. The first teep picked up a chair, while the second opted for a piece of brick wall. The third had a bowling ball, while the last student lifted what looked like a wicker basket, decidedly less impressive than the others.

'I take it the one on the end is the newbie,' Judd asked.

The man on the dais blew his whistle once more, and the first student moved their hands, sending the chair spinning in mid-air. Another whistle blow, and the brickwork splintered in the air, showering the ground with plaster, leaving a dozen single bricks floating in the air. The third spun their bowling bowl at speed, the finger holes blurring. The fourth whistle came, and the wicker basket remained floating. For a moment Judd thought they must have failed—until he looked closer. The tightly weaved wicker came apart, unravelling into one long thread.

Beside him, Lan laughed and gave a round of applause, which Judd couldn't help but join. The students either heard or sensed their appreciative audience, because they turned and gave a smile before showing off. Bricks juggled in formation; the chair started doing loop-the-loops.

For the first time, Judd's mind raced with what he could actually learn here. He didn't know what his power was. Surely that was worth staying to find out?

Lan looked back at him, smiling.

'It's not only practical lessons. We'll train you in international relations, business practices, negotiation, counter-intelligence, spy craft. We would take you from an average man with an average past and make you into something special.'

'To what end?' Judd asked.

She smiled. 'That's always up to you, Judd. It depends on what you want to do with your life. I can sense your hesitation, but honestly, we're a community, not a cult. Nobody gets asked to kill, and you don't have to work for the cause. Our kind have had a lot of bad press over the years. Some justified, most not.'

Judd frowned, looking back through the window. 'Not a cult,' he said, in a low voice. 'You dress in freaky uniforms, you train in counter-intelligence. There's a man in there unravelling wicker baskets with his mind.' He sighed. 'I dont know. I've spent my life trying to hide this from everyone I've ever met, so it's a bit of an about turn. Since I first discovered I had... this gift... I've never used it. Not once. I've not looked at what a bartender thinks as he pours me a beer, or what a beautiful woman thinks when I asked her out.'

'Not something we encourage here, either.'

'You know what I mean. I don't want this gift. If I could return it, I would. I certainly don't want to develop it to where I'm being flown into some war-torn country to pop a blood vessel in the brain of some warlord or other.'

'I already told you; it's not what this place is about. Well, okay, it's partly what this place is about. I won't lie to you and say that we develop people out of the goodness of our hearts—we have to look after ourselves. There's a certain amount of self-preservation required to having this gift. Mr Walker sees us as one family. He wants to give our kind the tools to go out into the world and be what we want to be, on our terms. You have a gift, one you can live with and have no one ever knowing, if you so choose. You could go right back to passing. A lot of us do. It's up to you. But isn't it better to know what you can do, and learn how to defend yourself, if you need to?'

He sighed, watching the students entertaining themselves with their gift.

'If you want to go, there's still a glide first thing in the morning,' Lan said. 'You can get on it, head back to your life out there. Or you can stay here.'

He looked into her face. There was no anger there, no disappointment. 'Tell me something,' he said. 'Were you monitoring me, before? When I left my room to explore, did you have to come find me?'

'Of course,' she said. 'You're going through the same thing as everyone else, Judd. People who go as long as you have without using their gifts, they don't want to let go of their fears, their prejudices. It's what's kept them alive this long. You weren't trying to run away, you were trying to find something to use against us. Something to prove you are right about us. Some terrible secret you could use to justify turning your back on this.' She leaned into him. 'Back when I got here, I did the same thing.'

Judd had no reply, but felt the heat of shame and anger spreading up his neck. How much of that had she pulled from his head? Or was that exactly as she was saying—his fear and prejudice?

She turned away, heading back the way they'd come. Judd looked back through the window. The woman with the bowling ball used it to destroy a series of paper targets, hitting each one through the heart.

'Lan,' he called after her, running down the corridor to catch her up. She stopped and turned back to wait for him. 'Last question. How the hell did Walker find me?'

She smirked her adorable smirk once more. 'You'll need to take it up with him. If you stick around, I'm sure he'd be happy to tell you. Listen, if you want to sneak around a bit, sneak around. Whatever you need to do, right?'

She turned away once more, and headed back down the corridor, leaving Judd surrounded by classrooms and his own fractured thoughts.

Chapter Ten

Neither of them had ever worked like this before. When they'd gone into Tijuana, they'd prepped the mission for months, setting up elaborate backstories, amassing a wealth of information to dissuade anyone looking at Lois's records from thinking she might be a rat. That level of cover was vital, not just as a safeguard but to get Lois mentally prepared. If she went into a situation knowing the background, knowing the key players, and with a backstory she could use, she had confidence—the confidence required to walk in the room in the first place. Unlike most of the other agents she'd met, she was not overly endowed with bravura or self-confidence. She had determination, curiosity, and faith in her handler, in the legend they created together. Here, whatever plan they went with, she walked in stripped of that confidence. With the stakes as high as they were, it left an uneasy gnawing at the pit of her stomach.

'The first option looks the best,' she said, staring at the displays on which Findlay had laid out three potential ways in.

'I agree,' he said, closing out the other two.

Sunset were actually looking for someone to come in and head up their corporate change committee, business-speak for working out who they could fire without affecting productivity. This was work Lois actually trained for, and as much as she hated it, it was an in they could achieve quickly. Her CV fit the bill, she was already living in the city and had links to the place already, something Sunset corporate encouraged. An agency, controlled by Interpol, would approach them with her as a candidate. She'd at least get an interview. Findlay had tech which would try to latch onto their servers while she was in the building, but neither of them held out much hope for that tactic—Sunset weren't likely to keep grizzly secrets on an unsecured network—but if it was all they could manage, it was better than nothing.

If she made the cut, she'd try to harvest as much data as she could. The good news was there was little for her to do. Just turn up and do a job. Findlay would get the data to tech experts who could sift through it, trying to find the needle in the haystack. All in one week.

One week. Then Sunset got the rubber stamp on their takeover of American Justice. If that happened, it didn't matter what Lois found.

Seven days. It was, frankly, a ludicrous ask. They may not even interview her until day eight.

'What do you think?' Findlay asked, once they'd gone through it for a third time, ironing out creases, running scenarios, trying to anticipate the mission's many failure points, most of which revolved around the fact Sunset's internal security would almost certainly notice their fast hacks into the mainframe.

'I think I'm probably going to end up dead in a ditch in the next seven days. I want to get Marisa and the girls out.'

'I agree with Marisa on this one. You send her and the girls away it looks suspicious, but if they stay, they're a huge validation point for you.'

'Why, because nobody would believe I'm idiot enough to put them in harm's way?'

'Precisely,' He said with a smirk. 'I've got them, okay. Nothing's going to happen to them.'

Lois scanned the data again, exhaling a long breath. 'Fuck it, let's do it.'

Findlay called up the dialler on his wrist. 'We're a go,' he said, and ended the call. Somewhere deep in the bowels of a French city, one of Interpol's agents would call Sunset to tell them all about a fantastic candidate they had.

'Here,' Findlay said, handing her a small package. 'Standard pad, completely unremarkable, except it's transmitting to me. Chances are they'll take it from you before the interview, but it'll still tell me where you are. Also, it'll be talking to the second item, which I want you to tape on the inside of your shirt. Sensors won't pick it up, but once you say, "it's a pleasure to meet you," it'll connect to the internal network and harvest data. Don't use it until you've cleared security and you're inside the building.'

'If they catch me?'

'Plead ignorance, say someone jostled you on the loop. It won't hold up to scrutiny but they likely won't execute you there in the building.'

'That's reassuring.'

'Well,' Findlay said. 'That covers it.'

'I guess so. At least we know one thing.'

'What's that?'

'It's not going to be a boring week.'

Chapter Eleven

'Captain?' Wyn called, poking her head into different quarters. 'Captain?'

'What's going on?' Hamza asked, as she moved past his pod.

'Fucking Ermine, man. Did you know about this?'

'About what?'

She waved him off and continued to move through the Minos.

'Wyn,' Hamza called after her. 'Cap's in his bunk, I think.'

Wyn did an about turn, heading back toward the bunks.

'What's going on?' Stef asked, emerging from the woman's bunk, pulling a shawl over her pyjama top.

'I need to talk to Captain Davis,' Wyn replied. 'Something's gone wrong with the nav calculations.... I...'

Her mind raced. She didn't want to break it to the crew until she had more facts. She certainly couldn't accuse the XO of sabotage without speaking to the Captain first, but there was no time to lose. The crew would need to speed up their prep. Shit, she needed to do her own. Should she head back to the flight deck and work out if she could reverse the changes? She hadn't heard a direct order, so it wouldn't technically be disobeying one. Miles couldn't order her to go to the toilet, let alone tell her she had to adhere to some magical new plan given to him by the XO.

Her job, her only job, was to get this ship, this crew, safely to the surface of Europa. To hell with what Sunset said. They weren't here.

She was still the fucking pilot.

'What's going on?' a voice croaked behind her.

Wyn whirled round to see the Captain, his normally impeccable hair tousled and eyes tired. He pulled on his overalls with the weary resignation of a parent dealing with a night terror. Still, his t-shirt didn't show a single crease as he buttoned the flight suit over it.

'I need to speak to you, sir. Privately.'

He nodded, running his hand through his hair. 'You've seen the new flight plan?'

Her heart sank.

If Davis knew about it, it was law.

'What new flight plan?' Stef asked.

'Cool your boots, Stef,' Davis replied, shooting her a look. 'We've been waiting for Wyn. Get the crew together. Five minutes. I'd hoped for more shut-eye before having to break the news, but there you go.'

He turned away, heading back to the mess. Wyn looked at Stef, who shrugged.

'You knew nothing about this?' Wyn asked.

'Nothing. Him and Ermine were in his ready room most of the day yesterday.'

Wyn's head swam. The cocktails the doc had pumped into her had left her brain messed up and woozy. She'd been rattling around like a bullet in a can with no idea what had been going on. 'Stef, how long was I out for?'

Stef scoffed. 'Three days. Hell of a power nap.' She pulled on the rest of her uniform and headed for the door. 'I hope you're rested,' she said, leaving Wyn in the bunk alone. 'I think you're going to need it.'

Five minutes later, the mood around the mess table a damn sight less jolly than the last time Wyn had been there. Li Wei brewed some tea. Wyn abstained. Nobody could even rouse themselves to the standard jokes about her being the only English woman to hate tea. She would have gone and fixed herself a coffee, but she was too angry.

Captain Davis entered, taking the empty seat at the end of the table. Zoe arrived a moment later, arms full of folders. She closed the door behind her. The last seat vacant was Ermine's—he took his customary standing position, leaning against the far wall. He hadn't said a word, and everyone knew better than to ask him anything.

'Thanks for coming,' Captain Davis said, his voice low and quiet. 'I understand there's some confusion, so I wanted to clarify. Yesterday, at seventeen hundred hours, we received an official mission directive from Control. They have run the numbers and feel they have a more optimal approach vector. One which gets us to Europa a few days early. There is an increased risk attached to the alternative course, but it's a risk which remains within operational norms. I have faith that with a bit of effort we can mitigate those risks further.'

'What's the added risk factor?' Stef asked. Her voice was icy, and she had a grim look on her face Wyn hadn't seen before. She looked pissed off. Wyn wasn't surprised. Stef's history with the Captain went back long before the Minos; he ran most things past her, used her as a sounding board, more than he did his XO, so it must chafe he'd kept secrets from her.

Around the table, those feelings echoed on the faces of the other crew. Everyone looked pissed, except Ermine. Well, he looked the normal level of pissed off he used as a baseline.

Captain Davis sighed and held his hands up. 'Look, I understand you're confused, upset. We'll get to that in a second, okay? I withheld this information from you, despite the advice of my XO. After having to make the call to sedate my pilot, I have to admit I was loath to say anything without her here.'

Wyn's stomach sank. It hadn't been Ermine. The Captain. He looked at her, trying to make eye contact, but she looked away, tears welling up.

'I received orders from Sunset and discussed them with the XO. I decided that rather than wake Wyn, I would input the course corrections personally. Wyn, I'd hoped to brief you in person, but there you go. You can't have everything. I wanted you to confirm before we briefed the crew. But we're pushing on time, so we need to commit to this new protocol.'

'Why?' Wyn asked. 'A few days aren't worth the extra risk.'

'Sorry,' Barnes said, putting his hand up like he was in class. 'I'd still like an answer to Stef's question.'

'The added risk is we arrive on the surface with a dramatically reduced magnetotail window to get under the ice,' Wyn replied, looking right at the Captain. He winced at her words.

Every face looked up.

'Jesus,' Stef said. 'How much shorter?'

'We'll have seven hours to get under the ice before we cook in our suits.'

A collective groan went round the table.

'We've run the calculation before with success,' Ermine said.

'Yeah,' Stef countered. 'At a much lower rate than the existing timescales.'

'This is what I don't get,' Wyn said. 'We've run this scenario before, dozens of times. We've rejected it every single time. The slingshots are too hard. The window is too tight. There are too many variables in here which don't work. So why, when we've had a plan in the bank for close to four years, do we get a correction with a few days left to go? It makes no sense. Especially not for the sake of shaving off a couple of extra sols.'

'It's not just a few extra sols,' Ermine said, leaning forward from the wall and placing his empty cup on the table. 'If we can shave two sols from the existing mission plan once we're on the surface, we can utilise an escape vector putting us on an exit from Jupiter's system with a much greater proximity to Saturn. It allows us to do a slingshot which knocks over three months off the return journey.'

He let it sink in for a moment. Three months off the return home wasn't nothing. They'd be pushing nine years on the mission by the time they got home. A length felt ever more as they reached the halfway point.

Ermine took his chair and looked at Wyn. 'Of course, you'd have worked it out for yourself if you'd done a bit of fact checking before stomping through the ship accusing everyone of mutiny.'

Heat crept up Wyn's neck, but she kept her voice calm. 'The slingshot manoeuvre is another thing we discounted in the planning stage. The Minos will face exposure to more of the Magnetotail than in the original plan. We don't know what it will do to hull integrity, especially when you add the increased g-force we'll be subjecting her to with two extreme slingshot moves. We could get down there and have the whole mission go swimmingly, and the fucking ship falls apart on the way home.'

'Things are getting worse back home,' Captains Davis said, in a low voice.

'Worse how?' Zoe asked.

'We calculated our mission prep based on the growth rates of the Mar. It gave us enough time to get there and back, mass-produce an antidote, and administer it while we still had crop functionality of around five percent globally. But the Mar's proliferation has only increased. Sunset and the WHO are keeping it quiet, but they've already reached five percent.'

Zoe's mouth dropped open, while the rest of the crew looked stricken.

'What does that mean?' Wyn asked.

'It means the mission is already a failure,' Zoe replied, in a low voice.

'It means,' the Captain added, 'the chances of getting home with a cure in time to make a difference are slim, but not non-existent. Mission control is adamant they can still turn the tide against the Mar. But every hour, every day, every minute we get home earlier increases the chances.'

The Captain sat back in his chair. He looked exhausted. The room fell silent as each of them contemplated the news.

The Mar.

What started as a bog standard tropical parasite in South America had used a perfect storm of rising temperatures and globalised trade to wend its merry way across the Earth, devastating everything in its path. The Mar targeted crops used in food production; it hit so hard and fast both the industrialised and non-industrialised nations of the world had no time to respond.

When the world had warmed, people had foreseen rising oceans, economic and real-world migrations to the previously third world, and irreparable damage to the world's ecosystems. Bad enough, and they did pretty much nothing to stop it. But they hadn't predicted the Mar.

By the time the world's scientists had launched the most ambitious scientific endeavour in history—the Minos—the planet's agricultural capacity had already reduced to ten percent of what it had been fifty years earlier, and had to feed a population nearly double the size. That was before you calculated the damage done to the wider ecosystems, and the way it had compounded co2 saturation. It was the worst thing, at the worst time.

The plan had been that the world would cling on to what it could long enough for the Minos and her crew to bring back the cure. From there, repopulation of the agricultural industries would take a few generations, but they could bring the world back from the brink.

This was why everyone around the table had given the best parts of their lives to this mission, even if they'd understood at the time it was a long shot. There wasn't another option. If this failed, humanity died. Not today, but within a few generations. Now, within touching distance of the cure, they might already be too late. The thin tendril of hope driving them this far seemed destined to wither and die in front of them.

'Thoughts?' Captain Davis asked.

'I understand the rationale,' Stef said, her voice calm. 'But if we're too late to make a difference, why the hell bust our asses and put us at graver risk? I'm not saying we wouldn't have agreed, but it would have been nice to have been at least consulted.'

'Exactly,' Barnes said. 'It feels like this conversation could have happened before you changed the mission, not after.'

'What the fuck do you care?' Ermine bit back. 'You're a fuck-ing medic, what difference does it make to you?'

'Because I volunteered for this mission the same as you did and I care about its success, can I fucking help you?'

'It matters,' the Captain said, raising his voice for the first time and flashing Ermine a stony stare that shut his second-in-com-mand up. 'Barnes, Stef, Zoe, Wyn, you're right. What can I say? This isn't a meritocracy, and we all get our orders. I take mine the same as you take yours. What's important is we achieve our mission. We can't do anything about what's going on back home. All we can do is our job. The question is, can we do it?'

He looked at Wyn.

'I don't know,' she said. 'Miles seems to think so. I need to check the data. If I hadn't been drugged, I could have been working on it hours ago.'

'You needed the sleep,' the Captain replied, shutting her com-plaint down. 'Li, Stef?'

A weight sank in Wyn's chest, the feeling of an admonished child. The discussion was over. No justice, no sympathy.

Across the table, Stef shrugged. 'We can start some prep ahead of time, try to shorten the deployment sequence once we're on the ice. If we're lucky, the ice won't be thicker than our estimates. I dunno. Perhaps.'

'Zoe?'

'Good to go. I'll focus primarily on sample collection and do the analysis on the return journey. I can lose a day of prep if needs be.'

'Okay,' the Captain said. 'Wyn, get to work. If the Minos can't do it, we need to know. But you'd better make damn sure she can. Hamza, you help her prep, work with Stef and Li. Any problems, you tell me immediately. Everyone else, I don't care what you have to do to make this work, you get it done. You need help, you ask. You get asked for help, you help. Understood?'

A series of nods went around the table, but the faces remained solemn. Wyn stood and poured herself a coffee, hoping nobody would try to talk to her. Thankfully, everyone was busy, so she made it back through to her flight module without having to lie about her seething anger.

'Okay, Miles,' she said, strapping herself into her flight chair. 'Let's see if the boffins at Sunset can tell their arses from their elbows.'

Through the glass, Jupiter loomed large, filling the entire view with angry red swirling gas storms. She'd been so absorbed in what was going on she'd scarcely noticed, but she noticed it now. She'd done nothing but study it for the past four years, but seeing it up close and personal was a different matter. The eye—raging, violent—was no more a static image. It looked alive, sweeping its gaze over them, daring them forward.

She blinked, tearing her gaze away.

'Show me what you've got.'

The screens filled with geometric lines, numbers, vectors. She tried not to focus on the planet beyond them, but failed. She shuddered and looked down at her pad.

Soon all that mattered were the numbers and the vectors. Not the planet below, not the mission change, not the goddamned XO.

She fell into the relaxing calm of computations, blocking everything else out, putting her mind to the task at hand. This was the only thing which ever gave her mind peace. She scribbled her own calculations, not trusting in the vectors or calculations Sunset had provided until she'd gotten there on her own and could verify them independently. She never trusted in anyone else's work. It had to be her own.

There was a knock at the door. Wyn looked up. She'd been working so long the lighting had adjusted to night settings without her noticing.

'Can I join you?' Captain Davis asked, a large cup of steaming coffee in his hand. Wyn felt the initial joy at his presence fade to a bitter hue as she remembered the meeting.

'Your ship,' she replied, turning back to the screens.

'Your deck,' he countered, placing the coffee in front of her and taking the empty co-pilot seat in a somewhat ungainly fashion. 'How are we looking?'

'I haven't finished my calculations yet.'

'Yes, but you already know...'

She shrugged. 'It'll be tight. I might be able to shave an additional hour off the entry to give us more time to get under the ice. But it's going to be a hell of a pull. I hope she's up to it.' She ran her knuckle along the front of the nav panel as she said this.

'She's got us this far.'

'This far is easy. Straight line.'

'We'll be fine.'

'If you say so.'

He paused a moment, weighing up whether to get into an argument or an apology with her, before deciding against either. Patting the arms of his chair, he eased himself up. 'I'll let you get on.'

He was at the door by the time Wyn's indignation finally burned out. 'Captain?' she asked.

'Yeah?'

'You inputted these approach vectors?' she asked.

'Ermine inputted them.'

'But they're your numbers?'

'I had to, Commander. I...'

'No, I wanted to say... good job.'

He gave her a warm smile, and left.

Wyn sighed, squinted at her pad, and went back to checking the numbers.

Chapter Twelve

The alarm startled him, unfamiliar as it was. Judd hadn't thought sleep would come for him last night, but the moment he resigned himself to wakefulness was the moment exhaustion reached him. He dreamed scattered dreams of fitful anxiety, dreams of spinning chairs and unravelling wicker, of brains in jars and implants and bloody noses. Some of it had been there in his head for years, he realised, always on the edge.

He brushed his teeth, appraising the man who stared back at him from the mirror. Pallid, doughy round the middle, he looked... soft. Maybe this was what he needed, in more ways than one. Regiment. Order. Wouldn't it be nice to look in the mirror and see a man worth looking at?

Washing his face, he ran his hands through his hair, and stared into his own eyes. Who the hell was he? A nobody. Wouldn't it be good to be... somebody?

He hated the man looking back at him, suddenly. He opened the drawers and found a pair of clippers inside. Methodically, he cut away at the mop of brown hair, staring himself down as he made every sweep over his head. When it was done, he ran his hands through the stubble, and smiled. Already he looked leaner, like a man determined. A man who could be... something.

Turning to the bed, he looked at the uniform left for him. Fuck it. Might as well go all in. When the chime on his door sounded, he was ready. He opened the door and found Lan stood on the other side. She gave him a wry smile, which made his heart skip a beat.

'Nice do. That mean you've decided?'

'Thought I'd give it a go.'

'Good man. Let's go get something to eat.'

Chapter Thirteen

Walking up the main steps of the Sunset headquarters building, she tried to ignore the sweat running down the back of her neck, and the near palpitations gripping her chest.

'Ms Pertin,' an officious-looking woman said, peering down her glasses at Lois as she strode across the enormous marble lobby to meet her. 'I'm Mrs Nord.'

'Pleased to meet you,' Lois replied, shaking the woman's hand. It felt like the corpse of a tiny bird had flopped briefly into her hand. 'This is a beautiful building.'

Mrs Nord offered a tight smile, which Lois knew instantly was the only kind to ever escape her face. 'A testament to the ability of the local marble merchants to see a mark coming when they see one.' She held out her hand for Lois's bag.

Lois offered a curt smile in return, and offered her bag. Immediately a small man appeared from behind a desk to take it from her.

Sand-coloured marble made up every surface, from the benches to the beams holding the roof in place. It was light, echoey, and ostentatious as hell. The sole exception to the endless marble were huge slabs of grey granite, each inscribed with a series of different languages. Lois wanted to ask what they were, but Mrs Nord was already retreating across the lobby, not in the mood to wait.

Lois caught up as quickly as she could, the clacking of her heels on the marble reverberating like a jackhammer across the open space.

'You're meeting with Carlos,' Mrs Nord said. 'He's the operational head of the company.'

This was a well-placed corporate role, but she hadn't expected her interview to be at that level. Of course, she knew all about Carlos. She tried to hide her surprise, which was a lot easier when the person you were talking to was power walking in the opposite direction. 'Any feedback you could offer me in terms of what to expect?' Lois asked.

Mrs Nord gave no response. They entered the lifts, and she placed her thumb on a biometric scanner, which automatically set their destination. They hurtled up the huge building in a clear glass bullet, unencumbered by sides, the air whooshing past them. Lois felt about an inch away from hurtling to her death. If she so much as reached out with her fingers she might lose them.

The doors opened on another huge atrium. Not quite so cavernous, but still imposing. It seemed as though the building was made of giant open spaces. Lois wondered where the hell the actual workers were.

At the far end of the room, a set of double doors opened, and a man utterly at peace with his world walked out. Dressed in the finest suit of dazzling emerald green, his skin artificially olive, his hair as jet black as his teeth were white, he strode across the room, his hand extended to greet Lois a good ten feet before it could meet hers. 'Ms Pertin,' he said, displaying his teeth to great effect. 'I'm Carlos.'

'It's a pleasure to meet you,' she replied, as much into the mic sewed into her jacket as to her proposed boss.

Before Lois could process the adrenaline coursing through her body at the knowledge she'd done something liable to get her shot on the spot, Carlos guided her out of the main atrium, not toward the huge double doors, but into a smaller room, much smaller. It reminded her of the interview rooms she'd taken perps apart in back on the beat. A million years ago, it seemed, but she recognised the setup, at least. Meant to both intimidate and put at ease. Intimate, but claustrophobic. One side was glass, looking out to the main atrium.

Carlos took the seat with its back to the window, Lois the one on the other side of the desk. They were high enough that wisps of cloud skipped across her view, and there was nothing to be seen of the city below.

'You have an impressive CV,' Carlos said, getting right down to business. He fished out a next gen pad, a tiny ball that erupted in light to bring up an interactive display. Lois had heard of their development, but hadn't ever actually seen one. 'Strange you've not crossed our path before.'

'Thank you,' she replied, trying to compose herself into a posture that would display her ease despite the total absence of it. 'Never in the right place at the right time, I guess.'

'Can you tell me a bit about your experience in change management?'

And with that, the nerves went away. All thoughts of the tech in her bag downstairs, of the mic broadcasting right this moment, it went away. She knew how to answer this. She wasn't a good undercover because she knew about tradecraft and signals and all that bullshit. She was a good undercover because corporate speak came as second nature. Without even having to dig too deep, she came up with two excellent examples from her past, tied them into the job description she'd already memorised, then led them back to a question for Carlos. The rapport between them grew, and she knew she had the job long before the meeting came to a close.

The door to the small office opened just as Carlos had moved onto telling Lois about the benefits package, and Mrs Nord reappeared.

'Mrs Burgess would like to see you, if you have a moment,' she said, in a whisper at full volume that seemed somewhat redundant to Lois.

'Of course,' Carlos said. 'Lois, I hope you don't mind?'

'No, go ahead,' Lois replied.

Carlos straightened his suit jacket as he stood, and walked around behind Lois to get to the door. Lois watched through the glass as he strode quickly across to the waiting woman. She was in her fifties, her blonde hair going grey in a rather handsome way. Even though Carlos was the chief operating officer of the company, meaning there was only one person above him in the food chain, there was a deference to the way he treated this woman. Interesting. Lois would have to look her up later, or at least have Findlay do so. She didn't recall coming across her in their research.

Burgess and Carlos had a brief conversation. Lois tried not to make it obvious she was watching.

Burgess looked directly at her, and Lois's blood ran cold.

She was blown.

If Carlos was shocked by whatever Burgess said to him, he didn't show it. He didn't look over at her at all, and when their conversation finished, he embraced his colleague and leaned in to kiss her cheek. Before Burgess left, she locked eyes with Lois once more, and the same chill buzzed down Lois's spine.

Fighting the urge to get up and sprint from the building, Lois remained in her chair, taking deep breaths without showing it, waiting for her interviewer to appear. Finally, he did so.

'Mrs Burgess is our head of security,' he said. 'I'm sure you'll be working closely with her, if you are to succeed.'

'I'd like that,' she replied. 'Stakeholder management is really what's core to this kind of role.'

'Well,' Carlos said, not sitting back down in his chair, signalling the meeting was over. 'I think we about wrapped it up anyway. Unless you have further questions?'

'No, I think it's about covered,' Lois replied, standing up as well.

'A pleasure to meet you,' Carlos said, displaying his teeth once more in a wide smile. 'We'll be in touch shortly.'

'I look forward to it,' Lois said.

Mrs Nord returned, ushering her out, back into the open lift. Lois braced for the moment she'd be shoved through the open side to plummet to her death. There were no pleasantries exchanged, and Lois was sure the pounding of her heart would be loud enough for the secretary to hear.

She was left in the main atrium and collected her bag, wondering why the hell she wasn't being led into a darkened room to be interviewed or tortured or killed, before heading back out in the cool Atlanta air.

Chapter Fourteen

The day passed in a blur. Lan stayed with him the whole day, giving him encouraging smiles when he failed to convey a message to the instructor in the first test, telling him things took time when the telekinesis test ended with him failing to make a feather move.

As the day went on, he couldn't help but feel more and more despondent as, one-by-one, another instructor failed to get a hint of The Gift out of him.

'Are you sure you've got it?' a grey-haired woman asked, as she peered over the top of her glasses; the same woman Walker had greeted at the gate the day before.

'I thought I did,' he mumbled.

'He's got it,' Lan said. 'Yesterday he skimmed a duel through a locked door. He's nervous.'

'Hmm,' the old lady said, peering into his eyes once more. 'Let's see. I'll drop my defences completely. Let's see what you can do. I'm thinking of an object. What is it?'

Clearing his mind, he peered into her eyes. Grey as her hair, and deep. So deep. They pulled on him, dragging him down.

Down.

Something was wrong.

He pulled back, trying to get away, but there was something... locked in. He couldn't look away from her, and something else, something dark, a shadow passing around his mind.

'What the hell?' he asked, but couldn't hear the words, like they'd dropped into a pit.

The shadow was in front of him. He could see it. Anger and fear rose up in him, and he stared it down.

A light grew inside him, starting in his chest, and he sensed something else. Discomfort? But not his. It belonged to the shadow invading his mind. He focused the glare of his light onto it, and there was another flash.

The connection broke, and he was back in the room, with the old woman, and with Lan.

The old woman looked terrified, and blood ran from Lan's nose.

'What happened?' he asked. The room swam as some part of his consciousness kept searching for the shadow, wanting to make sure it was gone.

'He's got power alright,' the old woman said, shakily.

'What the hell was that?' Lan asked, the question directed at the old woman, not Judd, and asked with no small note of fear.

'I don't know,' the old woman said. Not answering him directly, avoiding his eyes.

'Did I hurt you?' he asked, worried he'd fucked up somehow. What the hell had he done?

She gave a hollow little laugh. 'No, you didn't hurt me. I thought I'd take a look inside you and see if you do have the gift.

Normally it's something you'd be able to block, if you had the training. But this was something else. I'd like to have some more time with you, if I may, before I come to an assessment?'

'Um, sure, of course,' Judd replied.

'I'm Mrs. Smith,' she said, extending her hand to him. He took it. She looked him in the eyes once more, for a second. There was fear there.

'Not today, though. Lan, if you will?' She handed Lan a tissue.

'Sure,' Lan said. She wiped away the blood from her top lip, and tossed the tissue. She motioned for Judd to leave, and the two of them left Mrs. Smith to herself.

'Did I fuck something up in there?' Judd asked, as soon as they were outside the door.

Lan hushed him, and led him down the corridor until they were out of earshot. She peered around, and leaned in close. 'I have no idea what happened back there. I could tell what she was doing, a bit. She does it a lot to the new recruits. I don't like it much, myself. I think it's intrusive. But she's good at seeing what someone's talents are. It's not unusual for people on their first day to seize up. Nerves. Mrs. Smith can see what kind of gifts people have. But... I have no idea what happened in there. There was a flash of noise and light in my head, and I wasn't even connected to you. Whatever it is, I think you might have something we've never seen before. It was... it was like you had a light coming from you. Inside. I've honestly never seen anything like it before. Hey, this is exciting!'

'If you say so.' The sinking feeling in the pit of his stomach said that it was the opposite of exciting.

She flashed him another smile, reached into her pocket and took out a tissue, rubbing more blood away.

'Let's go see what's next, eh?'

There were more tests; not testing his gift, but testing him. Mental dexterity, IQ, general knowledge, education level, fitness, lung capacity, the list seemed endless. Judd grew exhausted as the day stretched on—the final test of the day on historical knowl-edge met with barely-syllabic responses.

'The, uh, data war.'

'Good,' the assessor, a man not much older than him but with an air of pugnacious arrogance, replied. 'It seems you have a grasp of the basics, at least. I suppose that's something.'

'Sorry. I'm pretty tired. It's been a long day.'

'Do you not think your stamina is something we're also trying to ascertain here?'

'What do you mean?' Judd asked, rubbing the bridge of his nose.

'Say you find yourself under interrogation. If there's one thing normals understand, it's that our power links to our mental stability. If they grind us down with hours of questioning, sleep deprivation, they can break us.'

'You're testing to see how I do when I'm tired? Well, I guess that pretty much fucks me, because I'm cranky when I'm tired.'

'So I see.'

'Are we done?'

'May I offer you a suggestion?' He arched his brow to indicate the suggestion would be coming, consent or no.

'Sure.'

'The sooner you stop fighting against this, the more rewarding you'll find it. And no, I didn't have to look into your mind to get that, in case you're wondering.'

'Well,' Judd said, getting up from his seat, the lactic acid in his legs still having not dissipated from hours before, 'you would say that, wouldn't you?'

He caught Lan giving the instructor an embarrassed smile of shared frustration, but didn't care. He wanted to go back to his bunk and sleep. Wordlessly, they both left the instructor's office.

'Are we done for the day?' he asked, a little too snappily.

'Yes,' Lan replied, her attempts to remain chipper fraying round the edges. 'Unless you want some dinner?'

'Sure.' He was, in fact, famished, something that hadn't occurred to him until she mentioned it, pulling back a curtain to reveal a gnawing emptiness in the pit of his stomach.

The dining room was busier than the night before. Blue-clad people of all denominations and creeds sat stuffed along the benches, some gossiping in low tones, some openly chatting away, others staring at each other in a way that seemed odd at first, until Judd realised they were speaking to each other in their heads, like he and Walker had up on the moon. Had they looked that lovesick? No wonder the barman acted weird.

Lan went to get food, and Judd sat at the end of a bench near the door, where the crowds were a little thinner. He stared at the table, tiredness washing over him. His eyes felt heavy.

'...kid who came in yesterday. I heard he flunked every single test today...'

'...I'm telling you, Walker's losing his touch if this is the dregs he's bringing in...'

'...the way he moons around after Lan, it's pathetic. I don't know how she stands...'

'...girl has a bigger tolerance for random assholes...'

The voices hit him in waves, mocking him and taunting him. He froze to the spot trying to work out where they came from, until he realised they were in his head. Except they weren't. Other people's heads, broadcasting to him. He'd spent the whole day not being able to hear anything—now he heard everything.

His stomach turned.

'...Such a loser, honestly...'

'...And that uniform? Didn't they have any that fit...'

'...They don't make them as tents...'

'...They might have to start...'

He stood, looking around him, wildly, trying to place the voices. People looked at him as though he'd screamed there was a fire in his pants.

One table away, huddled over their trays, shaking with laughter, sat a group of young men and women, half with their back to Judd, the others staring at at their plates.

Heat crept up Judd's neck. He looked around at the rest of the room. Some looked at him with disdain, some with confusion. Sweat beaded his forehead. He felt powerless, lost and at sea in a world he didn't know.

He'd have to do something. He thought of the moments at school feeling like this, how he'd always wished he'd stood up. Well, he was a man, wasn't he?

'I help you?' he called out to the table of gigglers. The rest of the canteen fell completely silent. All eyes were on him.

At the next table, a tall handsome man stood—a few years younger than Judd but with the confidence that good looks and toned muscles afforded. Even with a cursory glance Judd could see a bit of the arrogance of wealth thrown in for good measure.

'We're having a private conversation, between friends,' the boy said, crossing the room. 'Once you've been here a while, you'll learn there're things you should and shouldn't do. If you plan on sticking around. I heard there wasn't much point you being here.'

Judd stood, fists balled by his sides, a knot of bile tying his stomach up. He desperately searched for the perfect retort, but his brain was too tired once again.

'Stay away from me,' Judd said.

'That's all you've got?' the boy said. 'I've insulted you, in front of all these people. Shamed you, and...'

The heat in Judd's neck flashed, turning into something else. It grew. Swelled. Inside Judd was unlike anything he'd ever felt before—a bulb bursting with light. An incandescent heat. It grew in his chest until he couldn't keep it in there anymore. Couldn't help but let it out, spilling out of him with a roar. Light filled him, so bright, so hot.

Rage.

Locking eyes with the boy, he directed the light at him. The feeling of power as it flowed through him—the righteousness of it—felt exhilarating. Judd's fingers tingled as it flowed out of him, a release that felt almost euphoric, but wrapped in rage.

The light cleared, and Judd came back to himself, panting. Sweating. He looked around. Everyone in the canteen cowered. Whimpering. Crying. Screaming.

On the floor, blood smeared across his face, lay the boy. His eyes stared up at the ceiling, lifeless.

Lan stood before him, holding a tray of food in front of her. Tears were streaming down her cheeks, and the trickle of blood from her nose was back. She stared at Judd in open-mouthed horror. 'Judd,' she said. 'What did you do?'

Judd opened his mouth to speak, to say something, to explain, but something washed over him. He collapsed to his knees, tiredness enveloping him, and fell forward into darkness.

The story continues with
HANGING MOON

Grab the next thrilling installment of the
SUNSET CHRONICLES

SCAN ME

Leave a review

I really hope you've enjoyed reading *Fault & Fracture*.

If you did, the nicest thing you could do for me right now is to leave a review. Reviews are absolutely crucial to discoverability, and social proof. If you could take a second to rate and review this at the store of your choice, I'd hugely appreciate it.

Thanks,

Paul

Author's Note

I hope you're enjoying the first episodes of The Sunset Chronicles. Fault & Fracture is where things start to hot up, quite literally in the case of Judd. Make sure you pre-order your copy of Hanging Moon, where we'll find out what awaits Wyn on the ice and see what happens when Lois starts her new job at Sunset Industries. She's right, it's not going to be a boring week.

There are a number of influences at play in The Chronicles, but the telepathy aspect is an interesting one. The first novel I ever wrote to completion was a story about a telepathic boy whose path crosses with a serial killer, written back around 2007, the first time I ever gave serious effort to writing something from start to finish (I did it as my first attempt to do NaNoWriMo, the national novel-writing month I've since completed half a dozen times). I completed the novel on my then girlfriend's aunt's laptop, which waited for me to finish the whole thing, then immediately died, taking all those precious words with it. It's probably for the best, although as I write this, I've decided to revisit it. More on that soon.

One of the reasons I was interested in telepaths is because of one of the greatest Science Fiction series of all time — Babylon 5. I loved that show, but always felt that the moment the telepaths turned up in season five, the whole thing went off the rails. But what irked me (aside from the fact that Ivanova wasn't in it anymore) was the wasted potential of the telepath plot line. All the stuff about them being outcasts, pariahs, that was great. But why were they such whiny losers?

So, as I started to turn my attention to my own sci-fi epic (with great lashings of debt owed to J. Michael Straczynski's epic tale of shadows and grand forces) I was drawn back to where I had been the very first time I tried to tell a story from start to finish. To the idea of telepaths, to the potential inherent in a group of people reviled for their powers, but capable of managing that, of twisting the world to their end. There was strength in the idea of them, as well as vulnerability. They also provide a nice counter-point to the global greed of Sunset.

As always, there are a lot of people to thank, not least all the readers who've reached out to me to tell me how much they enjoyed book one, who left reviews, and who spread the word to their friends about this little project of mine.

But, as always, most of my thanks are for my family, who put up with me locking myself away in a little office for more time than is healthy, as well as putting up with the ridiculous music that gets blared from the same said office when I'm 'in the zone.'

This book is dedicated to my brother, Vince. I've never known such a voracious reader, and the words of encouragement he had for me when he read the Blood on the Motorway trilogy still pick me up when I'm struggling to get through a tricky patch. Love you, bro.

See you all at the hanging moon.

JOIN THE HOLLOW STONE

Join my reader's group
and be the first on the planet
to hear about new releases,
and get exclusive content
you won't find anywhere else.

GOT BLOOD?

An apocalyptic storm. A killer on the loose.
The battle for humanity's survival starts here.

Also by Paul Stephenson

BLOOD ON THE MOTORWAY

Blood on the Motorway
An apocalyptic storm. A killer on the loose. The battle for humanity's survival starts here.

Sleepwalk City
The fight for control has begun. Who will prevail in the battle for humanity's future in the pulse-quickening sequel to Blood on the Motorway?

A Final Storm
The sky is full of lights once more, and the survivors will need more than luck to get them through the coming storm. Who will survive, and who will thrive, in this heart-pounding finale to the Blood on the Motorway saga?

SUNSET CHRONICLES

Plague. Murder. Unrest. Humanity's future looks far from bright.

The year is 2107, and Earth is dying. For Wyn, Lois, and Judd, that's the least of their problems. Each holds a key to Earth's cure and humanity's survival in The Sunset Chronicles, the new sci-fi horror thrill-ride from Paul Stephenson, author of the bestselling British horror saga, Blood on the Motorway.

BLEAKWOOD

Introducing Bleakwood, a horror podcast from the creator of Blood on the Motorway and the Sunset Chronicles.

In the years since the fall, many of us have tried to find out why. To find what lead us here. But with so much of the old world gone, there are more questions than answers. What tore a hole in the world? Can we ever get it back?

But I think I've found something. A binder in the rubble. Don't ask me where. Full of stories about a little town called Bleakwood, stories that seem to show a way that....

They're not in any order, really. And I might be wrong. They might not have the answer. But I think it's in here.

A way back. To the before.

Listen, I'm just going to read them out, and you judge for yourself.

DARE YOU VENTURE INTO BLEAKWOOD?

WHAT TORE A HOLE IN THE WORLD?
CAN WE EVER GET IT BACK?

Find out in Bleakwood, the new horror podcast from the creator of Blood on the Motorway and The Sunset Chronicles

Created and narrated by Paul Stephenson and with stories by some of the most exciting voices in British modern Horror, subscribe to Bleakwood for a fresh story every month.

SCAN ME

www.ingramcontent.com/pod-product-compliance
Lightning Source LLC
Chambersburg PA
CBHW010743210726
48287CB00013B/2996